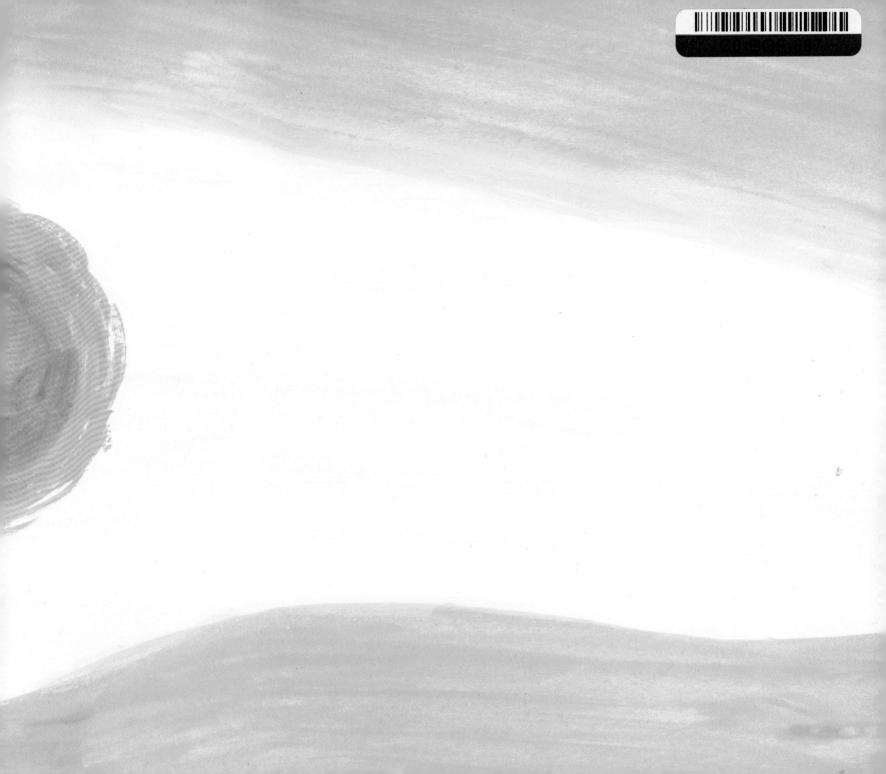

Smiling Eyes

Written by **Linda Sue Park**

Illustrated by **Lenny Wen**

Allida

An Imprint of HarperCollinsPublishers

Smiling eyes

bright eyes

twinkling eyes—
wink!

Shining eyes

Brown eyes

green eyes

hazel or blue

Crowds far and wide

and clouds
far above

Nearby

always

faces of love.

Purple frames
gold frames
round or square

Choosing new glasses—
look at this pair!

Eyes read
fingers read
print or braille

Mind's eye
teeming with
pictures and tales!

Worried eyes

sad eyes
warm salt tears

Tissues and
kisses and

wishes for cheer.

Open eyes
    close eyes
        squint in the sun

Sleepy eyes

dreamy eyes

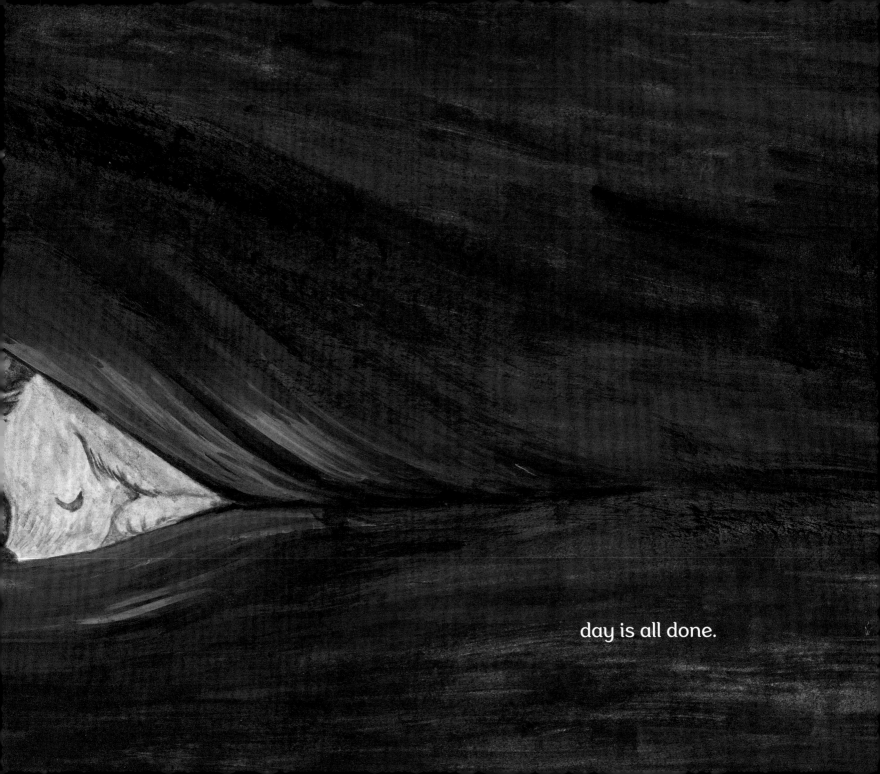

day is all done.

For Maya
—L.S.P.

For Anne, thank you for trusting me
with this wonderful book.
—L.W.